AND EVERY MORNING THE WAY HOME GETS LONGER AND LONGER

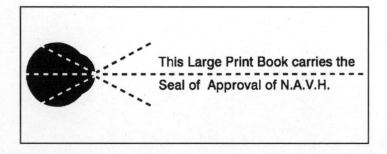

And Every Morning the Way Home Gets Longer and Longer

A Novella

Fredrik Backman

Translated by Alice Menzies

THORNDIKE PRESS
A part of Gale, Cengage Learning

GALE
CENGAGE Learning·

Farmington Hills, Mich • San Francisco • New York • Waterville, Maine
Meriden, Conn • Mason, Ohio • Chicago

GALE
CENGAGE Learning®

LIBRARY OF CONGRESS CATALOGING-IN-PUBLICATION DATA

Names: Backman, Fredrik, 1981– author. | Menzies, Alice, translator.
Title: And every morning the way home gets longer and longer : a novella / by Fredrik Backman ; translated by Alice Menzies.
Other titles: Och varje morgon blir vägen hem längre och längre. English
Description: Large print edition. | Waterville, Maine : Thorndike Press, 2017. | Series: Thorndike Press large print core
Identifiers: LCCN 2016045254| ISBN 9781410496836 (hardcover) | ISBN 141049683X (hardcover)
Subjects: LCSH: Large type books. | Psychological fiction.
Classification: LCC PT9877.12.A32 O3413 2017 | DDC 839.73/8—dc23
LC record available at https://lccn.loc.gov/2016045254

Published in 2017 by arrangement with Atria Books, an imprint of Simon & Schuster, Inc.

Printed in Mexico
1 2 3 4 5 6 7 21 20 19 18 17

Dear Reader,

One of my idols once said, "The worst part about growing old is that I don't get any ideas anymore." Those words have never quite left me since I first heard them, because this would be my greatest fear: imagination giving up before the body does. I guess I'm not alone in this. Humans are a strange breed in the way our fear of getting old seems to be even greater than our fear of dying.

This is a story about memories and about letting go. It's a love letter and a slow farewell between a man and his grandson, and between a dad and his boy.

I never meant for you to read it, to be quite honest. I wrote it just because I was trying to sort out my own thoughts, and I'm the kind of person who needs to see what I'm thinking on paper to make sense of it. But it turned into a small tale of how I'm dealing with slowly losing the greatest minds I know, about missing someone who is still here, and how I wanted to explain it all to my children. I'm letting it go now, for what it's worth.

It's about fear and love, and how they seem to go hand in hand most of the time. Most of all, it's about time. While we still have it. Thank you for giving this story yours.

Fredrik Backman

There's a hospital room at the end of a life where someone, right in the middle of the floor, has pitched a green tent. A person wakes up inside it, breathless and afraid, not knowing where he is. A young man sitting next to him whispers:

"Don't be scared."

Isn't that the best of all life's ages, an old man thinks as he looks at his grandchild. When a boy is just big enough to know how the world works but still young enough to refuse to accept it. Noah's feet don't touch the ground when his legs dangle over the edge of the bench, but his head reaches all the way to space, because he hasn't been alive long enough to allow anyone to keep his thoughts on Earth. His grandpa is next to him and is incredibly old, of course, so old now that people have given up and no longer nag him to start acting like an adult. So old that it's too late to grow up. It's not so bad either, that age.

The bench is in a square; Noah blinks heavily at the sunrise beyond it, newly woken. He doesn't want to admit to Grandpa that he doesn't know where they are, because this has always been their game: Noah closes his eyes and Grandpa takes him somewhere they've never been before. Sometimes the boy has to squeeze his eyes tight, tight shut while he and Grandpa change buses four times in town, and sometimes Grandpa just takes him straight into the woods behind the house by the lake. Sometimes they go in the boat, often for so long that Noah falls asleep, and once they've made it far enough Grandpa whispers "open your eyes" and gives Noah a map and a compass and the task of working out how they're going to get home. Grandpa knows he'll always manage, because there are two things in life in which Grandpa's faith is unwavering: mathematics and his grandson. A group of people calculated how to fly three men to the moon when Grandpa was young, and mathematics took them all the way there and back again. Numbers always lead people back.

But this place lacks coordinates; there are no roads out, no maps lead here.

Noah remembers that Grandpa asked him to close his eyes today. He remembers that they crept out of Grandpa's house and he knows that Grandpa took him to the lake, because the boy knows all the sounds and songs of the water, eyes open or not. He remembers damp wood underfoot as they stepped into the boat, but nothing after that. He doesn't know how he and Grandpa ended up here, on a bench in a round square. The place is strange but everything here is familiar, like someone stole all the things you grew up with and put them into the wrong house. There's a desk over there, just like the one in Grandpa's office, with a mini calculator and squared notepaper on top. Grandpa whistles gently, a sad tune, takes a quick little break to whisper:

"The square got smaller overnight again."

Then he starts whistling again. Grandpa seems surprised when the boy gives him a questioning look, aware for the first time that he said those words aloud.

"Sorry, Noahnoah, I forgot that thoughts aren't silent here."

Grandpa always calls him "Noah-noah" because he likes his grand-son's name twice as much as every-one else's. He puts a hand in the boy's hair, not ruffling it, just let-ting his fingers rest there.

"There's nothing to be afraid of, Noahnoah."

Hyacinths are blooming beneath the bench, a million tiny purple arms reaching up from the stalks to embrace the rays of sunlight. The boy recognizes the flowers, they're Grandma's, they smell like Christmas. For other children maybe that scent would be ginger biscuits and mulled wine, but if you've ever had a Grandma who loved things that grew then Christmas will always smell like hyacinths. There are shards of glass and keys glittering between the flowers, like someone had been keeping them safe in a big jar but then fell over and dropped it.

"What are all those keys for?" the boy asks.

"Which keys?" asks Grandpa.

The old man's eyes are strangely empty now. He raps his temples in frustration. The boy opens his mouth to say something, but stops himself when he sees that. He sits quietly instead and does what Grandpa taught him to do if he gets lost: take in his surroundings, look for landmarks and clues. The

bench is surrounded by trees, because Grandpa loves trees, because trees don't give a damn what people think. Silhouettes of birds lift up from them, spread out across the heavens, and rest confidently on the winds. A dragon is crossing the square, green and sleepy, and a penguin with small chocolate-colored handprints on its stomach is sleeping in one corner. A soft owl with only one eye is sitting next to it. Noah recognizes them too; they used to be his. Grandpa gave him the dragon when he had just been born, because Grandma said it wasn't suitable to give newborn children dragons as cuddly toys and Grandpa said he didn't want a suitable grandson.

People are walking around the square, but they're blurry. When the boy tries to focus on their outlines they slip from his eyes like light through venetian blinds. One of them stops and waves to Grandpa. Grandpa waves back, tries to look confident.

"Who's that?" the boy asks.

"That's . . . I . . . I can't remember, Noahnoah. It was so long ago . . . I think . . ."

He falls silent, hesitates, and searches for something in his pockets.

"You haven't given me a map and a compass today, nothing to count on, I don't know how I'm meant to find the way home, Grandpa," Noah whispers.

"I'm afraid those things won't help us here, Noahnoah."

"Where are we, Grandpa?"

Then Grandpa starts to cry, silently and tearlessly, so that his grandson won't realize.

"It's hard to explain, Noahnoah. It's so incredibly, incredibly hard to explain."

The girl is standing in front of him and smells like hyacinths, like she's never been anywhere else. Her hair is old but the wind in it is new, and he still remembers what it felt like to fall in love; that's the last memory to abandon him. Falling in love with her meant having no room in his own body. That was why he danced.

"We had too little time," he says.

She shakes her head.

"We had an eternity. Children and grandchildren."

"I only had you for the blink of an eye," he says.

She laughs.

"You had me an entire lifetime. All of mine."

"That wasn't enough."

She kisses his wrist; her chin rests in his fingers.

"No."

They walk slowly along a road he thinks he has walked before, not remembering where it leads. His hand is wrapped safely around hers and they're sixteen again, no shaking fingers, no aching hearts. His chest tells him he could run to the horizon, but one breath passes and his lungs won't obey him anymore. She stops, waits patiently beneath the weight of his arm, and she's old now, like the day before she left him. He whispers into her eyelid:

"I don't know how to explain it to Noah."

"I know," she says and her breath sings against his neck.

"He's so big now, I wish you could see him."

"I do, I do."

"I miss you, my love."

"I'm still with you, darling difficult you."

"But only in my memories now. Only here."

"That doesn't matter. This was always my favorite part of you."

"I've filled the square. It got smaller overnight again."

"I know, I know."

Then she dabs his forehead with a soft handkerchief, making small red circles bloom on the material, and she admonishes him:

"You're bleeding; you need to be careful when you get into the boat."

He closes his eyes.

"What do I say to Noah? How do I explain that I'm going to be leaving him even before I die?"

She takes his jaw in her hands and kisses him.

"Darling difficult husband, you should explain this to our grandson the way you've always explained everything to him: as though he was smarter than you."

He holds her close. He knows the rain will be coming soon.

Noah can see that Grandpa is ashamed the minute he says it's hard to explain, because Grandpa never says that to Noah. All other adults do, Noah's dad does it every day, but not Grandpa.

"I don't mean it would be hard for you to understand, Noahnoah. I mean it's hard for me to understand," the old man apologizes.

"You're bleeding!" the boy cries.

Grandpa's fingers fumble across his forehead. A single drop of blood is teetering on the edge of a deep gash in his skin, right above his eyebrow, sitting there fighting gravity. Eventually it falls, onto Grandpa's shirt, and two more drops immediately do the same, just like when children leap into the sea from a jetty, one has to be brave enough to go first before the others will follow.

"Yes . . . yes, I suppose I am, I must've . . . fallen," Grandpa broods as though that should have been a thought too.

But there are no silent thoughts here. The boy's eyes widen.

"Wait, you . . . you fell in the boat. I remember now! That's how you hurt yourself, I shouted for Dad!"

"Dad?" Grandpa repeats.

"Yeah, don't be scared Grandpa, Dad's coming to get us soon!" Noah promises as he pats Grandpa on the forearm, soothing him with a degree of experience far beyond what a boy his age should have.

Grandpa's pupils bounce anxiously, so the boy resolutely continues:

"Do you remember what you always said when we went fishing on the island and slept in the tent? There's nothing wrong with being a bit scared, you said, because if you wet yourself it'll keep the bears away!"

Grandpa blinks tightly, as though even Noah's outline has gotten blurry, but then the old man nods several times, his eyes clearer.

"Yes! Yes, so I did, Noahnoah, I said that, didn't I? When we were fishing. Oh, darling Noahnoah, you've grown so big. So very big. How is school?"

Noah steadies his voice, tries to swallow the trembling of his vocal cords as his heart pounds in alarm.

"It's fine. I'm top of the class in math. Just keep calm, Grandpa; Dad's going to come and get us soon."

Grandpa's hand rests on the boy's shoulder.

"That's good, Noahnoah, that's good. Mathematics will always lead you home."

The boy is terrified now, but knows better than to let Grandpa see that, so he shouts:

"Three point one four one!"

"Five nine two," Grandpa immediately replies.

"Six five three," the boy reels off.

"Five eight nine." Grandpa laughs.

That's another of Grandpa's favorite games, reciting the decimals of pi, the mathematical constant which is the key to calculating the size of a circle. Grandpa loves the magic of it, those key numbers which unlock secrets, open up the entire universe to us. He knows more than two hundred decimals of it by heart; the boy's record is half that. Grandpa always says that the years will allow them to meet in the middle, when the boy's thoughts expand and Grandpa's contract.

"Seven," says the boy.

"Nine," Grandpa whispers.

The boy squeezes his rough palm, and Grandpa sees that he is afraid, so the old man says:

"Have I ever told you about the time I went to the doctor, Noah-noah? I said, 'Doctor, Doctor, I've broken my arm in two places!' and the doctor replied, 'Then I'd advise you to stop going there!' "

The boy blinks; things are becoming increasingly blurred.

"You've told that one before, Grandpa. It's your favorite joke."

"Oh," Grandpa whispers, ashamed.

The square is a perfect circle. The wind fights in the treetops; the leaves move in a hundred dialects of green; Grandpa has always loved this time of year. Warm winds wander through the arms of the hyacinths and small drops of blood dry on his forehead. Noah holds his fingers there and asks:

"Where are we, Grandpa? Why are my stuffed animals here in the square? What happened when you fell in the boat?"

And then Grandpa's tears leave his eyelashes.

"We're in my brain, Noahnoah. And it got smaller overnight again."

Ted and his dad are in a garden. It smells like hyacinths.

"How is school?" the dad asks gruffly.

He always asks that and Ted can never give the right answer. The dad likes numbers and the boy likes letters; they're different languages.

"I got top marks for my essay," says the boy.

"And mathematics? How are you doing in mathematics? How are words meant to guide you home if you're lost in the woods?" the dad grunts.

The boy doesn't reply; he doesn't understand numbers, or maybe the numbers don't understand him. They've never seen eye to eye, his dad and him.

The dad, still a young man, bends down and starts pulling weeds from a flower bed. When he gets back up it's dark, though he could swear only a moment had passed.

"Three point one four one," he mumbles, but the voice no longer sounds like his own.

"Dad?" says the son's voice, but different now, deeper.

"Three point one four one! It's your favorite game!" roars the dad.

"No," the son softly replies.

"It was your . . ." the dad starts, but the air betrays his words.

"You're bleeding, Dad," says the boy.

The dad blinks at him several times, but then shakes his head and chuckles exaggeratedly.

"Ah, it's just a graze. Have I ever told you about the time I went to the doctor? I said, 'Doctor, Doctor, I've broken my arm. . . .' "

He falls silent.

"You're bleeding, Dad," the boy repeats patiently.

"I said, 'I've broken my arm.' Or no, wait, I said . . . I can't remember . . . it's my favorite joke, Ted. It's my favorite joke. Stop pulling at me, I can tell my favorite bloody joke!"

The boy carefully takes hold of his hands, but they're small now.

The boy's are like spades in comparison.

"Whose hands are these?" the old man pants.

"They're mine," Ted replies.

The dad shakes his head; blood runs from his forehead, anger fills his eyes.

"Where's my boy? Where's my little boy? Answer me!"

"Sit down a minute, Dad," Ted begs.

The dad's pupils hunt the dusk around the treetops; he tries to cry out but can't remember how; his throat will only give him hissing sounds now.

"How is school, Ted? How are you doing in mathematics?"

Mathematics will always lead you home. . . .

"You need to sit down, Dad, you're bleeding," the son begs.

He has a beard; it bristles beneath the dad's palm when he touches the boy's cheek.

"What happened?" whispers the dad.

"You fell over in the boat. I told you not to go out in the boat, Dad. It's dangerous, especially when you take No—"

The dad's eyes widen and he excitedly interrupts:

"Ted? Is that you? You've changed! How is school?"

Ted breathes slowly, talks clearly.

"I don't go to school anymore, Dad. I'm grown up now."

"How did your essay go?"

"Sit down now, please, Dad. Sit down."

"You look scared, Ted. Why are you scared?"

"Don't worry, Dad. I was just . . . I . . . you can't go out in the boat. I've told you a thousand times. . . ."

They aren't in the garden anymore; they're in an odorless room with white walls. The dad lays his hand on the bearded cheek.

"Don't be scared, Ted. Do you

remember when I taught you to fish? When we stayed in the tent out on the island and you had to sleep in my sleeping bag because you had a nightmare and wet yourself? Do you remember what I said to you? That it's good to wet yourself because it keeps the bears away. There's nothing wrong with being a bit scared."

When the dad sits down he lands on a soft bed, freshly made up by someone who isn't going to sleep there. This isn't his room. Ted is sitting next to him and the old man buries his nose in his son's hair.

"Do you remember, Ted? The tent on the island?"

"That wasn't me in the tent with you, Dad. It was Noah," the son whispers.

The dad lifts his head and stares at him.

"Who's Noah?"

Ted gently strokes his cheek.

"Noah, Dad. My son. You stayed in the tent with Noah. I don't like fishing."

"You do! I taught you! I taught you . . . didn't I teach you?"

"You never had time to teach me, Dad. You were always working. But you taught Noah, you've taught him everything. He's the one who loves math, like you."

The father's fingers grope around the bed; he's looking for something in his pockets, more and more frantically. When he sees that his boy has tears in his eyes, his own gaze flees toward the corner of the room. He clenches his fists until his knuckles turn white to stop them from shaking, mutters angrily:

"But what about school, Ted? Tell me how it's going at school!"

A boy and his grandpa are sitting on a bench in Grandpa's brain.

"It's such a nice brain, Grandpa," Noah says encouragingly, because Grandma always said that whenever Grandpa goes quiet, you just have to give him a compliment to get him going again.

"That's nice of you." Grandpa smiles and dries his eyes with the back of his hand.

"A bit messy though." The boy grins.

"It rained for a long time here when your Grandma died. I never quite got it back in order after that."

Noah notices that the ground beneath the bench has become muddy, but the keys and shards of glass are still there. Beyond the square is the lake, and small waves roll over it, memories of boats already passed. Noah can almost see the green tent on the island in the distance, remembers the fog which used to tenderly hug the trees like a cool sheet at dawn when they woke. Whenever Noah was scared of sleeping, Grandpa would take out a string and tie one end around his arm and the other around the boy's and promise that if Noah had nightmares he only had to pull on the string and Grandpa would wake up and bring him straight back to safety. Like a boat on a jetty. Grandpa kept his promise, every single time. Noah's legs dangle over the edge of the bench; the dragon has fallen asleep in the middle of the square, next to a fountain. There's a small group of tall buildings on the horizon on the other shore, amid the ruins of others which look like they've recently fallen down. The last ones standing are covered in blinking neon lights, strung here and there across their facades like they were taped up by someone who was either in too much of a hurry or absolutely desperate for a poo.

They wink patterns through the fog, Noah realizes, forming letters. "Important!" one of the buildings twinkles. "Remember!" says another one. But on the very tallest building, the one closest to the beach, the lights say, "Pictures of Noah."

"What are those buildings, Grandpa?"

"They're archives. That's where everything is kept. All the most important things."

"Like what?"

"Everything we've done. All the photos and films and all your most unnecessary presents."

Grandpa laughs, Noah too. They always give each other unnecessary presents. Grandpa gave Noah a plastic bag full of air for Christmas and Noah gave Grandpa a sandal. For his birthday, Noah gave Grandpa a piece of chocolate he'd already eaten. That was Grandpa's favorite.

"That's a big building."

"It was a big piece of chocolate."

"Why are you holding my hand so tight, Grandpa?"

"Sorry, Noahnoah. Sorry."

The ground around the fountain in the square is covered in hard stone slabs. Someone has scrawled advanced mathematical calculations all over them in white chalk, but blurry people are rushing this way and that across them and the soles of their shoes rub away the numbers one by one until only random lines remain, carved deeply into the stones. Fossil equations. The dragon sneezes in its sleep; its nostrils send a million scraps of paper covered in handwritten messages flying across the square. A hundred elves from a book of fairy tales Grandma used to read to Noah dance around the fountain trying to catch them.

"What's on those pieces of paper?" the boy asks.

"Those are all my ideas," Grandpa replies.

"They're blowing away."

"They've been doing that for a long time."

The boy nods and wraps his fingers tightly around Grandpa's.

"Is your brain ill?"

"Who told you that?"

"Dad."

Grandpa exhales through his nose. Nods.

"We don't know, really. We know so little about how the brain works. It's like a fading star right now — do you remember what I taught you about that?"

"When a star fades it takes a long time for us to realize, as long as it takes for the last of its light to reach Earth."

Grandpa's chin trembles. He often reminds Noah that the universe is over thirteen billion years old. Grandma always used to mutter, "And you're still in such a hurry to look at it that you never have time to do the dishes." "Those who hasten to live are in a hurry to miss," she sometimes used to whisper to Noah, though he didn't know what she meant before she was buried. Grandpa clasps his hands to stop them from shaking.

"When a brain fades it takes a long time for the body to realize. The human body has a tremendous work ethic; it's a mathematical masterpiece, it'll keep working until the very last light. Our brains are the most boundless equation, and once humanity solves it it'll be more powerful than when we went to the moon. There's no greater mystery in the universe than a human. Do you remember what I told you about failing?"

"The only time you've failed is if

you don't try once more."

"Exactly, Noahnoah, exactly. A great thought can never be kept on Earth."

Noah closes his eyes, stops the tears in their tracks, and forces them to cower beneath his eyelids. Snow starts to fall in the square, the same way very small children cry, like it had barely started at first but soon like it would never end. Heavy, white flakes cover all of Grandpa's ideas.

"Tell me about school, Noah-noah," the old man says.

He always wants to know everything about school, but not like other adults, who only want to know if Noah is behaving. Grandpa wants to know if the school is behaving. It hardly ever is.

"Our teacher made us write a story about what we want to be when we're big," Noah tells him.

"What did you write?"

"I wrote that I wanted to concentrate on being little first."

"That's a very good answer."

"Isn't it? I would rather be old than a grown-up. All grown-ups are angry, it's just children and old people who laugh."

"Did you write that?"

"Yes."

"What did your teacher say?"

"She said I hadn't understood the task."

"And what did you say?"

"I said she hadn't understood my answer."

"I love you," Grandpa manages to say with closed eyes.

"You're bleeding again," Noah says with his hand on Grandpa's forearm.

Grandpa wipes his forehead with a faded handkerchief. He's searching for something in his pockets. Then he looks at the boy's shoes, the way they swing a few inches above the tarmac with unruly shadows beneath them.

"When your feet touch the ground, I'll be in space, my dear Noahnoah."

The boy concentrates on breathing in time with Grandpa. That's another of their games.

"Are we here to learn how to say good-bye, Grandpa?" he eventually asks.

The old man scratches his chin, thinks for a long time.

"Yes, Noahnoah. I'm afraid we are."

"I think good-byes are hard," the boy admits.

Grandpa nods and strokes his cheek softly, though his fingertips are as rough as dry suede.

"You get that from your Grandma."

Noah remembers. When his dad picked him up from Grandma and Grandpa's in the evenings he wasn't even allowed to say those words to her. "Don't say it, Noah, don't you dare say it to me! I get old when you leave me. Every wrinkle on my face is a good-bye from you," she used to complain. And so he sang to her instead, and that made her laugh. She taught him to read and bake saffron buns and pour coffee without the pot dribbling, and when her hands started to shake the boy taught himself to pour half cups so she wouldn't spill any, because she was always ashamed when she did and he never let her feel ashamed in front of him. "The amount I love you, Noah," she would tell him with her lips to his ear after she read fairy tales about elves and he was just about to fall asleep, "the sky will never be that big." She wasn't perfect, but she was his. The boy sang to her the night before she died. Her body stopped working before her brain did. For Grandpa it's the opposite.

"I'm bad at good-byes," says the boy.

Grandpa's lips reveal all his teeth when he smiles.

"We'll have plenty of chances to practice. You'll be good at it. Almost all grown adults walk around full of regret over a good-bye they wish they'd been able to go back and say better. Our good-bye doesn't have to be like that, you'll be able to keep redoing it until it's perfect. And once it's perfect, that's when your feet will touch the ground and I'll be in space, and there won't be anything to be afraid of."

Noah holds the old man's hand, the man who taught him to fish and to never be afraid of big thoughts and to look at the night's sky and understand that it's made of numbers. Mathematics has blessed the boy in that sense, because he's no longer afraid of the thing almost everyone else is terrified of: infinity. Noah loves space because it never ends. It never dies. It's the one thing in his life which won't ever leave him.

He swings his legs, studies the glittering metals between the flowers.

"There are numbers on all the keys, Grandpa."

Grandpa leans forward over the edge and calmly looks at them.

"Yes, indeed, there are."

"Why?"

"I can't remember."

He suddenly sounds so afraid. His body is heavy, his voice is weak, and his skin is a sail about to be abandoned by the wind.

"Why are you holding my hand so tight, Grandpa?" the boy whispers again.

"Because all of this is disappearing, Noahnoah. And I want to keep hold of you longest of all."

The boy nods. Holds his grandpa's hand tighter in return.

He holds the girl's hand tighter and tighter and tighter, until she tenderly loosens one finger after another and kisses him on the neck.

"You're squeezing me like I was a rope."

"I don't want to lose you again. I couldn't go on."

She walks lightheartedly along the road next to him.

"I'm here. I've always been here. Tell me more about Noah, tell me everything."

His face softens bit by bit, until he's grinning and replies:

"He's so tall now, his feet are going to reach all the way to the ground soon."

"You'll have to put more stones under the anchor then," she says with a laugh.

His lungs force him to stop and lean against a tree. Their names are carved into the bark, but he doesn't remember why.

"My memories are running away

from me, my love, like when you try to separate oil and water. I'm constantly reading a book with a missing page, and it's always the most important one."

"I know, I know you're afraid," she answers and brushes her lips against his cheek.

"Where is this road taking us?"

"Home," she replies.

"Where are we?"

"We're back where we met. The dance hall where you stepped on my toes is over there, the café where I accidentally trapped your hand in the door. Your little finger is still crooked, you used to say that I probably only married you because I felt bad about that."

"I didn't care why you said yes.

Just that you stayed."

"There's the church where you became mine. There's the house that became ours."

He closes his eyes, lets his nose lead the way.

"Your hyacinths. They've never smelled so strong."

For more than half a century they belonged to one another. She detested the same characteristics in him that last day as she had the first time she saw him under that tree, and still adored all the others.

"When you looked straight at me when I was seventy I fell just as hard as I did when I was sixteen." She smiles.

His fingertips touch the skin above her collarbone.

"You never became ordinary to me, my love. You were electric shocks and fire."

Her teeth tickle his earlobe when she replies:

"No one could ask for more."

No one had ever fought with him like she had. Their very first fight had been about the universe; he explained how it had been created and she refused to accept it. He raised his voice, she got angry, he couldn't understand why, and she shouted, "I'm angry because you think everything happened by chance but there are billions of people on this planet and I found *you* so if you're saying I could just as well have found someone else then I can't bear your bloody mathematics!" Her fists had been clenched. He stood there looking at her for several minutes. Then he said that he loved her. It was the first time. They never stopped arguing and they never slept apart; he spent an entire working life calculating probabilities and she was the most improbable person he ever met. She turned him upside-down.

When they moved into their first house he spent the dark months growing a garden so beautiful that it knocked the air out of her when the light finally came. He did it with a determination only science can mobilize in a grown man, because he wanted to show that mathematics could be beautiful. He measured the angles of the sun, drew diagrams of where the trees cast their shade, kept statistics for the day-to-day temperatures, and optimized the choice of plants. "I wanted you to know," he said as she stood barefoot in the grass that June and cried. "Know what?" she asked. "That equations are magic, and that all formulas are spells," he said.

Now they are old and on a road. Her words against the fabric of his shirt:

"And then you went about growing coriander in secret every year, just to mess with me."

He throws out his arms in a gesture of innocence:

"I don't know what you're talking about. I forget things, you know,

I'm an old man. Are you saying you don't like coriander?"

"You've always known I hate it!"

"It must've been Noah. There's no trusting that boy." He laughs.

She stands on her tiptoes with both hands clutching his shirt and fixes her eyes on him.

"You were never easy, darling difficult sulky you, never diplomatic. You might even have been easy to dislike at times. But no one, absolutely no one, would dare tell me you were hard to love."

Next to the garden, which smelled of hyacinths and sometimes coriander, there was an old field. And there, right on the other side of the hedge, was a broken old fishing boat dragged up onto land by a neighbor many years earlier. Grandpa always said that he couldn't get any peace and quiet when he worked in the house, and Grandma always replied that she couldn't get any peace and quiet in the house when Grandpa was working there, so one morning Grandma went out into the garden and around the hedge and started to decorate the boat's cabin as an office. Grandpa sat there for years after that, surrounded by numbers and calculations and equations; it was the only place on Earth where everything was logical to him. Mathematicians need a place like that. Maybe everyone else does too.

There was a huge anchor leaning against one side of the boat. When

Ted was very small, the boy would occasionally ask his dad how long it would be before he was taller than it. The dad has tried to remember when it happened. He's tried so hard that the square in his head quaked. He learned his lesson; he was a different man when Noah was born, became someone else as Grandpa than he had been as a father. That's not unique to mathematicians. When Noah asked the same question Ted once had, Grandpa replied, "You'll have to hope it never happens, because only people who are shorter than the anchor get to play in my office whenever they want." And when Noah's head began to approach the top of the anchor, Grandpa placed stones beneath it so he would never lose the privilege of being disturbed.

"Noah has gotten so smart, my love."

"He always has been, it just took you awhile to catch up," she snorts.

His voice catches in his throat.

"My brain is shrinking now, the square gets smaller every night."

She strokes his temples.

"Do you remember what you said, when we first fell in love, that sleeping was a torment?"

"Yes. Because we couldn't share our sleep. Every morning when I blinked awake, the seconds before I knew where I was were unbearable. Until I knew where you were."

She kisses him.

"I know that the way home is get-ting longer and longer every morn-ing. But I loved you because your brain, your world, was always big-ger than everyone else's. There's still a lot of it left."

"I miss you unbearably."

She smiles, her tears on his face.

"Darling stubborn you. I know you never believed in life after death. But you should know that I'm dearly, dearly, dearly hoping that you're wrong."

The road behind her is blurry, the horizon bearing rain. He holds her as hard as he can. Sighs deeply.

"Lord how you'll argue with me then. If we meet in Heaven."

A rake has been left propped

against a wall. Lying next to it are three plant markers flecked with damp earth. On the ground, there's a bag with a pair of glasses sticking out of one of its pockets. A microscope has been forgotten on a footstool and there's a white coat hanging from a hook, a pair of red shoes visible beneath. Grandpa proposed to her here, by the fountain, and Grandma's things are still everywhere.

The boy carefully touches the lump on Grandpa's forehead.

"Does it hurt?" he asks.

"No, not really," Grandpa replies.

"I mean on the inside. Does it hurt on the inside?"

"It hurts less and less. That's one good thing about forgetting things.

You forget the things that hurt too."

"What does it feel like?"

"Like constantly searching for something in your pockets. First you lose the small things, then it's the big ones. It starts with keys and ends with people."

"Are you scared?"

"A bit. Are you?"

"A bit," the boy admits.

Grandpa grins.

"That'll keep the bears away."

Noah's cheek is resting against the old man's collarbone.

"When you've forgotten a person, do you forget you've forgotten?"

"No, sometimes I remember that I've forgotten. That's the worst kind of forgetting. Like being locked out in a storm. Then I try

to force myself to remember harder, so hard that the whole square here shakes."

"Is that why you get so tired?"

"Yes, sometimes it feels like having fallen asleep on a sofa while it's still light and then suddenly being woken up once it's dark; it takes me a few seconds to remember where I am. I'm in space for a few moments, have to blink and rub my eyes and let my brain take a couple of extra steps to remember who I am and where I am. To get home. That's the road that's getting longer and longer every morning, the way home from space. I'm sailing on a big calm lake, Noahnoah."

"Horrible," says the boy.

"Yes. Very, very, very horrible. For

some reason places and directions seem to be the first thing to disappear. First you forget where you're going, then where you've been, and eventually where you are . . . or . . . maybe it was the other way around. . . . I . . . my doctor said something. I went to my doctor and he said something about, or did I say something. I said: 'Doctor, I . . .' "

He raps his temples, harder and harder. The square moves.

"It doesn't matter," the boy whispers.

"Sorry, Noahnoah."

The boy strokes his arm, shrugs.

"Don't worry. I'm going to give you a balloon, Grandpa. So you can have it in space."

"A balloon won't stop me from disappearing, Noahnoah." Grandpa sighs.

"I know. But you'll get it on your birthday. As a present."

"That sounds unnecessary." Grandpa smiles.

The boy nods.

"If you keep hold of it you'll know that right before you went into space someone gave you a balloon. And it's the most unnecessary present anyone can get because there's absolutely *no* need for a balloon in space. And that'll make you laugh."

Grandpa closes his eyes. Breathes in the boy's hair.

"That's the best present I've never been given."

The lake glitters, their feet move

from side to side, trouser legs fluttering in the wind. It smells like water and sunshine on the bench. Not everyone knows that water and sunshine have scents, but they do, you just have to get far enough away from all other smells to realize it. You have to be sitting still in a boat, relaxing so much that you have time to lie on your back and think. Lakes and thoughts have that in common, they take time. Grandpa leans toward Noah and breathes out like people do at the start of a long sleep; one of them is getting bigger and one of them is getting smaller, the years allow them to meet in the middle. The boy points to a road on the other side of the square, blocked off by a barrier and a big warning sign.

"What's happened there, Grandpa?"

Grandpa blinks several times with his head against the boy's collarbone.

"Oh . . . that road . . . I think it's . . . it's closed. It washed away in the rain when your Grandma died. It's too dangerous to think about now, Noahnoah."

"Where did it go?"

"It was a shortcut. It didn't take long at all to get home in the mornings when I took that road, I just woke up and there I was," Grandpa mumbles and raps his forehead.

The boy wants to ask more, but Grandpa manages to stop him.

"Tell me more about school,

Noahnoah."

Noah shrugs.

"We don't count enough and we write too much."

"That's always the way. They never learn, the schools."

"And I don't like the music lessons. Dad's trying to teach me to play guitar, but I can't."

"Don't worry. People like us have a different kind of music, Noahnoah."

"And we have to write essays all the time! The teacher wanted us to write what we thought the meaning of life was once."

"What did you write?"

"Company."

Grandpa closes his eyes.

"That's the best answer I've

heard."

"My teacher said I had to write a longer answer."

"So what did you do?"

"I wrote: Company. And ice cream."

Grandpa spends a moment or two thinking that over. Then he asks:

"What kind of ice cream?"

Noah smiles. It's nice to be understood.

He and the girl are on a road and they're young again. He remembers each of the very first times he saw her, he hides those pictures as far from the rain as he can. They were sixteen and even the snow was happy that morning, falling soap-bubble light and landing on cold cheeks as though the flakes were gently trying to wake someone they loved. She stood in front of him with January in her hair and he was lost. She was the first person in his life that he couldn't work out, though he spent every minute of it after that day trying.

"I always knew who I was with you. You were my shortcut," Grandpa confides.

"Even though I never had any sense of direction." She laughs.

"Death isn't fair."

"No, death is a slow drum. It counts every beat. We can't haggle with it for more time."

"Beautifully said, my love."

"I stole it."

Their laughter echoes in each

other's chests, and then he says:

"I miss all our most ordinary things. Breakfast on the veranda. Weeds in the flower beds."

She takes a breath, then answers:

"I miss the dawn. The way it stamped its feet at the end of the water, increasingly frustrated and impatient, until there was no more holding back the sun. The way it sparkled right across the lake, reached the stones by the jetty and came onto land, its warm hands in our garden, pouring gentle light into our house, letting us kick off the covers and start the day. I miss you then, darling sleepy you. Miss you there."

"We lived an extraordinarily ordinary life."

"An ordinarily extraordinary life."

She laughs. Old eyes, new sunlight, and he still remembers how it felt to fall in love. The rain hasn't arrived yet.

They dance on the shortcut until darkness falls.

People are moving back and forth across the square. A blurry man steps on the dragon's foot, the dragon gives him a telling off. A boy is playing guitar beneath a tree, a sad tune, Grandpa hums along. A young woman walks barefoot across the square, stops to stroke the dragon. Her palms suddenly search her red coat, finding something in her pockets, something she seems to have spent a long time looking for. She looks up, straight at Noah, laughs happily and waves. As though he helped her to look, and she wants him to know he can stop now. That she's found it. That everything's okay. For a single moment he sees her face clearly. She has Grandma's eyes. Then the boy blinks, and she's gone.

"She looked like . . ." he whispers.

"I know." Grandpa nods, his hands move anxiously in his own pockets, then he lifts them up and lets his fingers move against his temples, like the outside of a box of raisins. Like he's trying to shake loose a piece of the past in there.

"I . . . she . . . that's your grandma. She was younger. You never got to meet her young, she

has . . . she had the strongest feelings I ever experienced in a person, when she got angry she could empty a full bar of grown men, and when she was happy . . . there was no defending yourself against that, Noahnoah. She was a force of nature. Everything I am came from her, she was my Big Bang."

"How did you fall in love with her?" the boy asks.

Grandpa's hands land with one palm on his own knee and one on the boy's.

"She got lost in my heart, I think. Couldn't find her way out. Your grandma always had a terrible sense of direction. She could get lost on an escalator."

And then comes his laughter,

crackling and popping like it's smoke from dry wood in his stomach. He puts an arm around the boy.

"Never in my life have I asked myself how I fell in love with her, Noahnoah. Only the other way around."

The boy looks at the keys on the ground, at the square and the fountain. He glances up toward space; if he stretches his fingers he can touch it. It's soft. When he and Grandpa go fishing they sometimes lie in the bottom of the boat with their eyes closed for hours without saying a word to one another. When Grandma was here she always stayed at home, and if anyone asked where her husband and grandson were she always said, "Space." It belongs to them.

It was a morning in December when she died. The whole house smelled of hyacinths and the boy cried the whole day. That night he lay next to Grandpa on his back in the snow in the garden and looked up at the stars. They sang for Grandma, both of them. Sang for space. Have done the same almost every night since. She belongs to them.

"Are you scared you're going to forget her?" the boy asks.

Grandpa nods.

"Very."

"Maybe you just need to forget her funeral," the boy suggests.

The boy himself could well imagine forgetting funerals. All funerals. But Grandpa shakes his head.

"If I forget the funeral I'll forget why I can't ever forget her."

"That sounds messy."

"Life sometimes is."

"Grandma believed in God, but you don't. Do you still get to go to Heaven if you die?"

"Only if I'm wrong."

The boy bites his lip and makes a promise:

"I'll tell you about her when you forget, Grandpa. First thing every morning, first of all I'll tell you about her."

Grandpa squeezes his arm.

"Tell me that we danced, Noah-noah. Tell me that that's what it's like to fall in love, like you don't have room for yourself in your own feet."

"I promise."

"And tell me that she hated coriander. Tell me that I used to tell waiters in restaurants that she had a serious allergy, and when they asked whether someone could really be allergic to coriander I said: 'Believe me, she's seriously allergic, if you serve her coriander you could die!' She didn't find that funny at all, she said, but she laughed when she thought I wasn't looking."

"She used to say that coriander was a punishment rather than a herb." Noah laughs.

Grandpa nods, blinks at the treetops, and takes deep breaths from

the leaves. Then he rests his forehead against the boy's and says:

"Noahnoah, promise me something, one very last thing: once
your good-bye is perfect, you have
to leave me and not look back. Live
your life. It's an awful thing to miss
someone who's still here."

The boy spends a long time thinking about that. Then he says:

"But one good thing with your
brain being sick is that you're going to be really good at keeping
secrets. That's a good thing if
you're a grandpa."

Grandpa nods.

"That's true, that's true . . . what
was that?"

Both of them grin.

"And I don't think you need to

be scared of forgetting me," the boy says after a moment's consideration.

"No?"

The corners of the boy's mouth reach his earlobes.

"No. Because if you forget me then you'll just get the chance to get to know me again. And you'll like that, because I'm actually a pretty cool person to get to know."

Grandpa laughs and the square shakes. He knows no greater blessing.

They're sitting on the grass, him and her.

"Ted is so angry at me, love," Grandpa says.

"He's not angry at you, he's angry

at the universe. He's angry because your enemy isn't something he can fight."

"It's a big universe to be angry with, a never-ending fury. I wish that he . . ."

"That he was more like you?"

"Less. That he was less like me. Less angry."

"He is. Just sadder. Do you remember when he was little and asked you why people went into space?"

"Yes. I told him it was because people are born adventurers, we have to explore and discover, it's our nature."

"But you could see that he was scared, so you also said: 'Ted, we're not going into space because we're afraid of aliens. We're going because we're scared we're alone. It's an awfully big universe to be alone in.' "

"Did I say that? That was smart of me."

"You probably stole it from some-one."

"Probably."

"Ted might say the same thing to Noah now."

"Noah has never been afraid of space."

"That's because Noah is like me, he believes in God."

The old man lies down on the grass and smiles at the trees. She gets up and walks past the hedge, along the side of the boat, stroking it thoughtfully.

"Don't forget to put more stones under the anchor, Noah is growing so quickly," she reminds him.

The boat's cabin, the room in which he worked for so many years, looks so small in the twilight. Even though there was space for all his biggest thoughts. The lights are still there, the ones he strung up in a tangle on the outside of the boat so that Noah could always find his way if he woke up from a nightmare and needed to find his grandpa. A chaotic mess of green, yellow, and purple bulbs, as though Grandpa had been desperate for a poo when he put them up, so Noah would start laughing when he saw them. You can't be afraid of crossing dark gardens if you're laughing.

She lies down next to him, sighs with his skin close to hers.

"This is where we built our life. Everything. There's the road where you taught Ted to ride a bike."

His lips vanish between his teeth when he admits:

"Ted taught himself. Like he taught himself to play guitar after I told him to stop messing about with it and do his homework instead."

"You were a busy man," she whispers, regret filling every word because she knows she bears the same guilt.

"And now Ted is a busy man," he says.

"But the universe gave you both Noah. He's the bridge between

you. That's why we get the chance to spoil our grandchildren, because by doing that we're apologizing to our children."

"And how do we stop our children from hating us for that?"

"We can't. That's not our job."

He chases his breaths between throat and chest.

"Everyone always wondered how you put up with me, my love. Sometimes I wonder too."

Her giggles, how he misses them, the way they seemed to gain speed all the way from her feet.

"You were the first boy I met who knew how to dance. I thought it was probably best to seize the opportunity; who knows how often boys like that turn up?"

"I'm sorry about the coriander."

"No you're not, not at all."

"No, not at all, actually."

She carefully lets go of his hand in the darkness, but her voice still rests in his ear.

"Don't forget to put more stones under the anchor. And ask Ted about the guitar."

"It's too late now."

She laughs inside his brain then.

"Darling obstinate you. It's never too late to ask your son about something he loves."

Then the rain starts to fall, and the last thing he shouts to her is that he also hopes he's wrong. Dearly, dearly, dearly hopes. That she'll argue with him in Heaven.

■ ■ ■ ■

A boy and his dad walk down a corridor; the dad holds the boy's hand softly.

"It's okay to be afraid, Noah, you don't need to be ashamed," he repeats.

"I know, Dad, don't worry," Noah says and yanks up his trousers when they slip down.

"They're a little bit too big; that was the smallest size they had. I'll have to adjust them for you when we get home," the dad promises.

"Is Grandpa in pain?" Noah wants to know.

"No, don't worry about that, he just cut his head when he fell over in the boat. It looks worse than it is, but he's not in pain, Noah."

"I mean on the inside. Does it hurt on the inside?"

The dad is breathing through his nose, and his eyes are closed; his steps slow down.

"It's hard to explain, Noah."

Noah nods and holds his hand more tightly.

"Don't be scared, Dad. It'll keep the bears away."

"What will?"

"Me wetting myself in the ambulance. That'll keep the bears away. There won't be any bears in that ambulance for years!"

Noah's dad's laugh is like a rumble. Noah loves it. Those big hands gently holding his small ones.

"We just need to be careful, does that make sense? With your grandpa. His brain . . . the thing is, Noah, sometimes it's going to be working slower than we're used to. Slower than Grandpa is used to."

"Yeah. The way home's getting longer and longer every morning now."

The father squats down and hugs him.

"My wonderful smart little boy. The amount I love you, Noah, the sky will never be that big."

"What can we do to help Grandpa?"

The dad's tears dry on the boy's sweatshirt.

"We can walk down the road with him. We can keep him company."

They take the lift down to the hospital parking lot, walk hand in hand toward the car. Fetch the green tent.

Ted and his dad are arguing again. Ted begs him to sit down, the dad furiously bellows:

"I don't have time to teach you to ride your bike today, Ted! I told you! I have to work!"

"It's okay, Dad. I know."

"For God's sake, I just want my cigarettes! Tell me where you've hidden my cigarettes!" the dad roars.

"You stopped smoking years ago," says Ted.

"How the hell would you know?"

"I know because you stopped

when I was born, Dad."

They stare at one another and breathe. Breathe and breathe and breathe. It's a never-ending rage, being angry at the universe.

"I . . . it . . ." Grandpa mumbles.

Ted's big hands hold his thin shoulders; Grandpa touches his beard.

"You've gotten so big, Tedted."

"Dad, listen to me, Noah is here now. He's going to sit with you. I just need to get a few things from the car."

Grandpa nods and rests his forehead against Ted's forehead.

"We need to go home soon, my boy, your mother's waiting for us. I'm sure she's worried."

Ted bites his lower lip.

"Okay, Dad. Soon. Really, really soon."

"How tall are you now, Tedted?"

"Six foot one, Dad."

"We'll have to put more stones under the anchor when we get home."

Ted is almost at the door when Grandpa asks if he has his guitar with him.

There's a hospital room at the end of a life where someone, right in the middle of the floor, has pitched a green tent. A person wakes up inside it, breathless and afraid, not knowing where he is. A young man sitting next to him whispers:

"Don't be scared."

The person sits up in his sleeping

bag, hugs his shaking knees, cries.

"Don't be scared," the young man repeats.

A balloon bounces against the roof of the tent; its string reaches the person's fingertips.

"I don't know who you are," he whispers.

The young man strokes his forearm.

"I'm Noah. You're my grandpa. You taught me to cycle on the road outside your house and you loved my grandma so much that there wasn't room for you in your own feet. She hated coriander but put up with you. You swore you would never stop smoking but you did when you became a father. You've been to space, because you're a born adventurer, and once you went to your doctor and said, 'Doctor, doctor! I've broken my arm in two places!' and then the doctor told you that you should really stop going there."

Grandpa smiles then, without moving his lips. Noah places the string from the balloon in his hand and shows him how he is holding the other end.

"We're inside the tent we used to sleep in by the lake, Grandpa, do you remember? If you tie this string around your wrist you can keep hold of the balloon when you fall asleep, and when you get scared you just need to yank it and I'll pull you back. Every time."

Grandpa nods slowly and strokes

Noah's cheek in wonder.

"You look different, Noahnoah. How is school? Are the teachers better now?"

"Yes, Grandpa, the teachers are better. I'm one of them now. The teachers are great now."

"That's good, that's good, Noah-noah, a great brain can never be kept on Earth," Grandpa whispers and closes his eyes.

Space sings outside the hospital room; Ted plays guitar; Grandpa hums along. It's a big universe to be angry at but a long life to have company in. Noah strokes his daughter's hair; the girl turns toward him in the sleeping bag without waking up. She doesn't like mathematics, she prefers words and

instruments like her grandpa. It won't be long before her feet touch the ground. They sleep in a row, the tent smells like hyacinths, and there's nothing to be afraid of.

ABOUT THE AUTHOR

Fredrik Backman is the *New York Times* bestselling author of *A Man Called Ove, My Grandmother Asked Me to Tell You She's Sorry,* and *Britt-Marie Was Here.* His books have been published in more than thirty-five countries. He lives in Stockholm, Sweden, with his wife and two children.